Thomas W. Balch

The Brooke Family of Whitchurch, Hampshire, England

together with an account of Acting-governor Robert Brooke of Maryland

and Colonel Ninian Beall of Maryland and some of their descendants

Thomas W. Balch

The Brooke Family of Whitchurch, Hampshire, England
*together with an account of Acting-governor Robert Brooke of Maryland and
Colonel Ninian Beall of Maryland and some of their descendants*

ISBN/EAN: 9783337262921

Printed in Europe, USA, Canada, Australia, Japan

Cover: Foto ©Raphael Reischuk / pixelio.de

More available books at **www.hansebooks.com**

THE BROOKE FAMILY

OF

WHITCHURCH, HAMPSHIRE, ENGLAND

THE BROOKE FAMILY

OF

WHITCHURCH, HAMPSHIRE, ENGLAND

TOGETHER WITH AN ACCOUNT OF

ACTING-GOVERNOR ROBERT BROOKE

OF MARYLAND

AND

COLONEL NINIAN BEALL

OF MARYLAND

AND SOME OF THEIR DESCENDANTS

BY

THOMAS WILLING BALCH

PHILADELPHIA
PRESS OF ALLEN, LANE & SCOTT
1899

PREFACE.

In this small book I have sought to present infor-
mation I have gathered about Acting-Governor Robert
Brooke of Maryland and his family in England, and
Colonel Ninian Beall of Maryland : I have given also
an account of *some* of their descendants. My father,
Mr. Thomas Balch, left family papers containing much
valuable material, to which Mrs. Henry Irvine Keyser
of Baltimore, Maryland, and Arthur Spayd Brooke,
Esq. of Reading, Pennsylvania, have added most
kindly from their family archives. I am indebted also
for some important facts to Mrs. Jane Baldwin of
Annapolis, Maryland, and for kind aid to Gregory B.
Keen and John Woolf Jordan, Esquires, of the Historical Society of Pennsylvania. I searched carefully
in the archives of the Maryland Land Office, and
in September, 1897, I visited Whitchurch in Hants,
England. The drawings of the coats of arms I owe
to the kindness of Mr. Brooke.

THOMAS WILLING BALCH.

PHILADELPHIA, December 1st, 1898.

THE BROOKE FAMILY OF WHITCHURCH

AND

SOME OF THEIR DESCENDANTS.

———◆◆◆———

THE little village of Whitchurch is situated in the
northern part of Hampshire, England. Since Saxon
times the place has always had a church built of the
white stone found in the neighborhood; and thus the
name—Whitchurch—originated. In the latter half of
the sixteenth century there lived at Whitchurch, Richard Brooke, gentleman, and his wife, Elizabeth Twyne.[1]
That they were people of means for those days is
shown by the items in the will of Richard Brooke
dividing among his children his "leases held by the
Blessed Trinity in Winchester," his lease of Knoll,
his woods in Chalgrove and Freefolk and the Manor
of West Fosbury. To his wife he leaves his "free
lands and tenements in Whitchurch and Freefolk"

---

[1] She was sister and co-heir of John Twyne of Whitchurch, and appears to have descended from Sir Bryan Twyne of Long Parish, County
Southampton, who was living before 1500.

Twyne *Arms :* Ar. a fesse, embattled, sable, in chief two estoiles of
the last. William Berry's *County Genealogies. Hants.* London, 1833,
pages 222, 223, 339.

and his "lease of the parsonage of Whitchurch," their homestead.[2]

This house is built of brick in the open country a short distance beyond the church, which is at the western end of the village.   In September, 1897, it still stood firm and sound, but with an addition on the side towards the open country away from the church and the village.   In the old part there were three rooms on the lower floor.   The biggest room, which served probably both as a reception and dining room, contained a large open fireplace.   The room back of this, very likely, was the kitchen.   In the small remaining room, perhaps the stairs stood.   In the largest room on the upper floor, also possessed of a fine open fireplace, Charles the First passed a few days during the Civil War before the battle of Newberry in 1644.   The brasses of Richard Brooke and his wife, together with

---

[2] Will dated January 10th, 1588-9, as of Richard Brooke of Whitchurch, County Southampton, Gentleman.   Proved May 6th, 1594, by Elizabeth Brooke, relict and executrix.

Will of Elizabeth Brooke dated May 16th, 1599.   Proved by Robert Brooke, son and executor, in the Prerogative Court of Canterbury and recorded in the Principal Registry of Probate at London.

Communicated by Arthur Spayd Brooke, Esq.

Brooke *Arms:* Chequy or and az. on a bend gu. a lion, passant, of the first.   *Crest*—A demi lion, rampant, erased, or.   The use of these arms was confirmed by a patent by William Camden, Clarencieux, Visitation of 1634.   William Berry's *County Genealogies. Hants.* London, 1833, page 339.

two smaller ones underneath of their three sons and three daughters, respectively, the whole surmounted by the Brooke and the Twyne arms, are affixed on the wall near one corner ; all these brasses originally were upon the floor of the church. Under the brasses a brass plate bears the following inscription, which I copied myself :

" PIETATIS OPUS.

" This grave (of griefe) hath swallowed up with wide
    and open mouth,

The bodie of good Richard Brooke, of Whitchurch,
    Hampton South

And Elizabeth his wedded wife, twice twentie yeares
    and one,

Sweete Jesus hath their soules in heaven, ye ground
    flesh, skin and bone.

In Januarie (worne with age) daie sixteenth died hee,

From Christ full fifteene hundred yeares and more by
    ninetie three,

But death her twist of life in Maie, daie twentith did
    untwine

From Christ full fifteen hundred yeares and more by
    ninetie nine.

They left behinde them well to live, and growne to
    goode degree,

First, Richard, Thomas, Robert Brooke, the youngest
    of the three,

Elizabeth, and Barbara, then Dorathee the last,

All six the knot of Natures love, and kindnes keeping fast,

This Toome stone with the Plate thereon, thus graven
fare and large

Did Robert Brooke, the youngest sonne, make of his
proper charge.

A Citizen of London State, by faithful service free,

Of Marchantes, greate adventurers, a brother sworne
is hee,

And of the Indian Companie (come gaine or losse) a
limb,

And of the Goldsmithe liverie, All these Godes giftes
to him :

This Monument of memorie in love performed hee ;

December thirtie one, from Christ sixteene hundred
and three :

       "Anno Domini 1603: Laus Deo."

Richard and Elizabeth Brooke, as the inscription
in the church tells us, were married in 1552 and had
six children in all :

    Thomas Brooke who married Susan Forster,
    Richard who died without issue,
    Dorothy who married Richard Venables,
    Elizabeth,
    Barbara,
    Robert, a citizen of London, who married Mary Duncomb
      and had issue.

Thomas Brooke of Whitchurch, gentleman, the eldest son was born in 1560. He matriculated at New College, Oxford, November 24th, 1581, received the degree of B. A. May 4th, 1584, and was barrister at law in the Inner Temple in 1595; he sat for Whitchurch Borough in the Parliament that was summoned to meet at Westminster March 19th, 1603-4, and was dissolved February 9th, 1610-11, and died in 1612.[3] He married Susan Forster.

Symonds[4] in his diary of the marches of the Royal Army thus describes a monument erected to their memory.

" Whit-church Church.

" Against the north wall chancel, a faire monument, the statue of a man in a barr-gowne, and a woman:
  " Thom. Brooke, Ar. etat. 52, ob. 13 Sep. 1612.
  " Susanna uxor ejus, filia natu max. Thomae Forster Militis in parochia Hunsdon com. Hertf. [one of the Judges K. B. Mons. Insc. at Hunsdon].

[3] *Alumni Oxonienses*, by Joseph Foster, London, 1891; early series, Vol. I.

Members of Parliament. Ordered, by The House of Commons, *to be printed* 1st March, 1878. Part I., page 445.

[4] *Diary of the Marches of the Royal Army during the great Civil War, kept by Richard Symonds, now first published from the original MS. in the British Museum. Printed for the Camden Society,1859*, page 141.

" Quarterly, 1 and 4, Checky, or and azure, on
a bend gules a lion passant or [Brooke];
2 and 3, Argent, a fess embattled sable, in
chief two estoils of the second [Twyne];
impaling.

" Quarterly, 1, and 4, a chevron vert between
three bugle-horns, sable [Forster]; 2 gone;
3 Argent, on a bend sable three martlets
or.   *Crest*, on a wreath azure and or, a demi-
lion erased or." [5]

The monument is in the belfry, and is made of the
stone of the neighborhood.   They lie outstretched
side by side; their heads, collars, hands, and cuffs are
white; the rest of their dress is black, except that the
middle of her gown in front from top to bottom is a
light red.

Susan Forster's father, Sir Thomas Forster, was
born about 1569, and belonged to the Forster family of
Northumberland; [6] he was spoken of first in 1587 as

· *Diary of the Marches of the Royal Army during the great Civil War,
kept by Richard Symonds, now first published from the original MS. in
the British Museum.   Printed for the Camden Society, 1859*, page 142.
The additions in brackets were made by the Editor, Charles Edward
Long, M. A.

' *The Judges of England*, by Edward Foss, London, 1857; Vol. VI.,
157.

Sir Thomas Forster was the son of Thomas Forster of Hunsdon in
Co. Hertford, and grandson of Roger Forster of the Forsters of North-

Forster of Iden Sussex.

Forster of Middlesex and Battel C. Sussex.

a barrister in both Coke's and Croke's Reports ; he
became a reader of the Society of the Inner Temple in
1596 ; he was called on November 24th, 1607, to the
bench as judge of the Common Pleas, and sat in that
Court for four years and a half; he died May 18th,
1612, and was buried at Hunsdon, in Herefordshire.
Thomas Sutton named him one of the first governors of
his hospital—the Charter House.[7]   His youngest son,
Robert Forster, was created January 27th, 1640, judge
of the Common Pleas, but as he adhered during the
Civil War to the Royal cause, he was deposed from
the bench.   After the restoration, Charles the Second
recalled him to his seat, and on October 21st, 1660,
appointed him Chief-Justice of the King's Bench ;
this office he held until his death, October 4th, 1663.
He was buried in the church at Egham.[8]

umberland. *Arms :* Quarterly, first and fourth, ar. a chev. vert, between three bugle horns, stringed, sa. ; second, ar. on a bend sa. three
martlets or ; third, ar. on a bend engr. sa. three stags' heads cabossed or.—
Crest : A stag, statant, sa. horned or. William Berry's *County Genealogies. Sussex.* London 1830, page 192.
   The wife of Sir Thomas Forster was Susan Forster, daughter of Thomas
Forster of Iden in Co. Sussex, and of St. John's Street, London. *Ib.*,
page 192.

 [7] *10 Coke's Reports,* 10*a.*

 [8] *The Judges of England,* by Edward Foss, London, 1864 ; Vol. VII.,
97-99.
   Alumni Oxonienses, by Joseph Foster, London, 1891 ; early series,
Vol. II.

Symonds in his diary thus speaks of Charles the First's stay at the Brooke house :

"Friday, 18 October, 1644.

*   *   *   *   *   *   *

"This night the King lay at the White hart in Andevor ; the whole army in the feild.

"Satterday, as soone as light, the army marched after the enemy. The King lay at Whitchurch at Mr. Brookes his howse that night.

*   *   *   *   *   *   *

"Munday 21 October. His Majestie, &c. left Whitchurch, the generall rendesvouz upon the Downe near Kingsmill's howse [at Sidmonton]."[9]

Thomas and Susan Brooke had[10]

---

[9] Symonds's *Diary of the Marches of the Royal Army During the great Civil War*, pages 141, 142.

[10] Extract from the *Parish Register* at Whitchurch :

"*1612*. Benjamin Brooke was baptized Sept 17 [brother of Robert the emigrant].

"*1612*. Thomas Brooke Esq' was burried Sept. 17th. Susan Brooke his wife was burried the 18th day of Sept 1612. Both are burried beneath the monument.

"*1612*. Thomas the sonne of Thomas Brooke Esq' was baptized March the 16 by Wm. Harding Vicar.

"*1613*. Thomas son of Thos. Brooke Esq' was burried Januarie the 22 by John Belchamber Vicar.

"*1653*. Thomas son of Thomas and Mary Brooke was baptized Nov. 2, 1653."

"*1665*. Thomas Brooke Esq' was burried Jan 25 killed by lightening Jan 24 near Winton [Winchester].

"*1674*. Mrs. Mary Brooke was buried July 29 [wife of Thomas Brooke killed in 1665].

Communicated by the Rev. H. Edmund Sharpe of Whitchurch and Arthur Spayd Brooke Esq.

1. Thomas Brooke of Whitchurch, the eldest son. He matriculated at Oriel College, Oxford, October 27th, 1615, aged sixteen years, and was barrister at law in the Inner Temple in 1623 as of Whitchurch, Hants, gentleman.[11]

2. Richard Brooke.

3. Robert Brooke, who emigrated to Maryland in 1650.

4. John Brooke, who matriculated at Wadham College Oxford, May 11th, 1621, aged sixteen years.[12]

5. William Brooke.

6. Humphry Brooke, who was a citizen of London.

7. Charles Brooke.

8. Susan Brooke, who married William Havers of Thelveton Hall, Co. Norfolk.

9. Elizabeth Brooke.

10. Frances Brooke.

11. Benjamin Brooke, who died young.

Robert Brooke, the third son of Thomas Brooke and Susan Forster, matriculated at Wadham College, Oxford, April 28th, 1618 ; he received his B. A. July 6th, 1620, and M. A. April 24th, 1624.[13] He married February 25th, 1627, his first wife, Mary Baker, daughter of Thomas Baker, of Battel, Sussex.[14] In

[11] *Alumni Oxonienses*, by Joseph Foster, London, 1891, early series, Vol. I.

[12] *Ib.*, Vol. I.

[13] *Ib.*, Vol. I.

[14] Thomas Baker was the son of
John Baker, of Battel, eldest son of
John Baker, of Duckings, or Ducking-house, in Withyham, son and heir, temp. Hen. VIII. (1509-1547) of
Henry Baker, of Battel, eldest son, temp. Henry VII. (1485-1509) of
Thomas Baker, of Battel, son and heir, temp. Edw. IV. (1461-1483) of

1635 he married his second wife, Mary Mainwaring
(see page 59). He left the following memoran-
dum of himself and his family, which Roger Brooke
Taney, one of his descendants and of his second wife,
Mary Mainwaring, gives in his autobiography.[15]

"Robert Brooke was born at London, 3d June,
1602, being Thursday, between 10 and 11 of the
clock in the forenoon, being Corpus Christi Day.

"Mary Baker, born at Battel in Sussex.

"Robert Brooke and Mary Baker intermarried
1627, the 25th of February, being St. Matthias' Day
and Shrove Monday.

"1. Baker Brooke, eldest son to Robert and Mary
Brooke, was born at Battel, November the 16th, being

John Baker, of Battel, son and heir, temp. Henry VI. (1422-1461) of
John Baker, of Battel, son and heir, temp. Henry IV. (1399-1413) of
Simon Baker, of Battel, son and heir, temp. Rich. II. (1377-1399) of
John Baker, of Battel, in Co. Sussex, 49 Edw. III., 1375.

Arms: Ar. a tower, between three keys, erect, sa.

Crest: On a tower, sa. an arm, embowed, in mail, holding in the hand
a flint-stone, ppr.

A pedigree of this family, with the above coat and crest, under the
hand of Sir Richard St. George, Clarencieux, was produced at the Visitation of Kent in 1619. William Berry's *County Genealogies, Sussex.*
London 1830, pages 225, 226.

[15] *Memoir of Roger Brooke Taney, LL. D., Chief Justice of the
Supreme Court of the United States 1836-1864.* By Samuel Tyler, LL. D.,
of the Maryland Bar. Baltimore 1872, pages 22-25. Chief Justice Taney
was born March 17, 1777, in Calvert Co., Md. He was the son of Michael
Taney and Monica Brooke, daughter of Roger Brooke, the third in succession from Robert Brooke, the emigrant. (*Ib.,* 20, 21). He died in
1864.

Baker of Battel
Sussex

Mainwaring of
Cheshire

Brooke of Whitchurch
Hampshire

Sunday, at half hour past 9 o'clock in the morning, being new moon the night before, and was baptized the 2d day of December following, his Uncle Thomas Brooke, and his Grandfather Baker, his Godfathers, and his Aunt Foster, wife to Mr. Robert Foster, his Godmother, 1628.

"2. Mary Brooke, eldest daughter to Robert Brooke and Mary his wife, was born 1630, at Battel, the 19th day of February, being Saturday, between 2 and 3 of the clock in the afternoon, the moon being new the next day, and was baptized the Sunday following, her Godfather Mr. Thomas Foster, of Battel, and her Godmothers her Grandmother Baker and her Cousin Heath.

"3. Thomas Brooke, second son to Robert Brooke and Mary his wife, was born at Battel, 1632, the 23d day of June, being Saturday, a quarter of an hour past 2 o'clock in the morning, and was baptized the 3d day of July following, his Godfathers Mr. Christopher Dow Dean, of Battel, and Mr. Thomas Bryan, of Battel, his Godmother Mrs. Eliza Foster, wife of Mr. Goddard Foster.

"4. Barbara Brooke, second daughter to Robert Brooke and Mary his wife, born at Whickham.

"May the 11th, 1635, Robert Brooke (aforementioned) was married to Mary, second daughter to

Roger Mainwaring, Doctor of Divinity and Dean of Worcester, which Mary was born at St. Giles-in-the-Fields, London.

"1. Charles Brooke, eldest son of Robert Brooke and Mary his wife, was born at St. Giles-in-the-Fields, Middlesex, 3d April, 1636, between 11 and 12 o'clock in the forenoon, being Sunday, and was baptized the day following, his Grandfather, the Bishop of St. David's and his Uncle Townley, his Godfathers, and his Aunt Stedney his Godmother, under ♃ Jupiter 3 min.

"2. Roger Brooke was born the 20th September, 1637, at Bretnock College, between 11 and 12 o'clock at night, it being Wednesday, and was baptized the following day, his Godfathers the Bishop of St. David's and his Uncle Stevens, and his Aunt Sarah Mainwaring his Godmother, ♃ under Jupiter [see page 61].

"3. Robert Brooke was born at London, in St. Brides' Parish, April 21st, 1639, half an hour before 1 of the clock in the morning, it being Sunday and new moon two days after, his Godfather my Cousin Thomas Foster (♃ under Jupiter), son to Serecant Foster and my Cousin William Brooke, and his Godmother my sister Elizabeth.

"4. John Brooke, born at Battel, the 20th September, 1640, being Sunday, between 1 and 2 o'clock in the afternoon, his Godfather William Jackson, D. P., and his Godmother Mrs. Jackson.

"5. Mary Brooke was born at Battel the 14th day of April, being Thursday, 1642, after 1 o'clock in the morning, the moon being in the last quarter the Tuesday before, her Godfather Mr. Jackson, and her Godmother old Mrs. Beneford.

"6. William Brooke, born at Battel the 1st day of December, 1643, between 11 and 12 o'clock at night, the moon being new in the morning at 5, and baptized the same day, his Godfather Mr. March and his Godmother Mrs. Pound.

"7. Ann Brooke, born at Bretnock, 22d January, 1645, between 5 and 6 of the clock at night, being Thursday, her Godfather the Bishop of St. David's, his Deputy her Uncle Henry Mellyne, her Godmothers Mrs. Mary Mainwaring and Mrs. Jones, ♀ under Venus.

"8. Francis Brooke, born at Horwett in Hantshire, the 30th May, 1648, being Tuesday, between 11 and 12 o'clock, at noon, ☽ under Luna.

"The before-named Robert Brooke, Esquire, arrived out of England in Maryland the 29th day of June, 1650, in the 48th year of his age, with his wife and ten children. He was the first that did seat the Patuxent, about twenty miles up the river at De la

Brooke, and had one son there, born in 1651, called Basil, who died the same day. In 1652 he removed to Brooke Place, being right against De la Brooke; and on the 28th of November, 1655, between 3 and 4 o'clock in the afternoon, had two children Eliza and Henry, twins. He departed this world the 20th day of July, and lieth buried at Brooke Place Manor ; and his wife, Mary Brooke, departed this life the 29th November, 1663."[16]

On September 20th, 1649, Lord Baltimore commissioned Robert Brooke commander of a new county in Maryland with full powers to levy and command troops, grant commissions, hold court, etc. This commission was in part as follows: " Cecilius Absolute Lord and Proprietary of the Provinces of Maryland and Avalon Lord Baron of Baltimore, &c². to our right trusty and well beloved William Stone, Esqr. our Lieutenant of the said Province of Maryl^d.

    *   *   *   *   *   *   *

Greeting whereas our trusty and well Beloved Robert Brooke Esqr. doth this next Summers Expedition intend to transport himself his Wife Eight

------

[16] " The foregoing is a true copy taken from my grandfather's book of his own handwriting and his eldest son Baker after his decease, this 2nd day of October 1710, by me

ROGER BROOKE."

This Roger Brooke married Elizabeth Hutchins (see page 62.) Communicated by Arthur Spayd Brooke, Esq.

Sons and family and a Great Number of other Persons into our said Province of Maryland there to erect make and settle a Considerable Plantation now we having good Experience of the Honour worth and abilities of the said Robert Brooke and of his faithfulness to us and his real desires and intentions for the Good and Prosperity of our said Province Know yee that we do hereby Constitute and appoint him the said Robert Brooke to be Commander under us and our heirs and our and their Lieutenant of the said Province for the time being of one whole County within our said Province of Maryland to be newly set forth erected Nominated and Appointed for that Purpose," etc.[17]   At the same time Lord Baltimore appointed Robert Brooke a member of the Privy Council of Maryland.[18]   In 1650 he came over to Maryland in his own ship bringing his wife, children, and a large number of servants with him, forty persons in all,[19] and arrived at the end of June.   On October 3rd following, Charles County on the Patuxent River was created and Robert Brooke named Commander.[20]

[17] *Archives of Maryland: Proceedings of the Council of Maryland, 1636-1667.* Baltimore, 1885, pages 237, 238.

[18] *Ib.*, 240, 241.

[19] *Ib.*, 256.

[20] *Ib.*, 259, 260.

The Commissioners of the Council of State for the Commonwealth of England, who were sent over to reduce the Old Dominion to the authority of the Parliament, by a proclamation of March 29th, 1652, deposed William Stone from the governorship of Maryland, and until they reinstated him on the 28th of June following, they named Robert Brooke Acting-Governor. In their proclamation they said: "That the said Council of Maryland or any two or more of them whereof Robert Brooke Esqr to be one do Govern and direct the Affairs thereof and hold Courts as often as they think fit for that purpose."[21] When Governor Stone was reinstated, Robert Brooke was continued on the Council.

Thomas Brooke, the second son of Robert Brooke and Mary (née Baker) Brooke, was born at Battel, England, June 23rd, 1632, and came over to Maryland with his father. On June 3d, 1658, the Council of Maryland commissioned him a Captain in the Maryland forces,[22] and on February 11th, 1660. the following commission signed by Philip Calvert, raised him to the rank of Major:

"Com" issued to Cap" Thomas Brookes to be Maior

[21] *Archives of Maryland: Proceedings of the Council of Maryland, 1636-1667.* Baltimore, 1885, pages 271, 272.

[22] *Ib.*, pages 344-346.

of the Regiment now under Comand of Coll[l] W[m] Euans and power to inlist for his owne Company such and so many of the Jnhabitants from George Reads on the Southside and S[t] Leonards Creeke on the Northside to the head of Patuxent Riuer, as hee shall thinke fitt Giuen &c Vnder my hand and lesser Seale of the said Province this 11th day of ffebr 1660. with power to choose his own officers of his ffoote Company.

"P. C."[23]

On June 14th, 1661, Thomas Brooke was appointed a commissioner for Calvert County;[24] September 15th, 1663, he was elected a Burgess of the County,[25] and April 20th, 1666, he was named Sheriff of the County.[26] The General Assembly appointed Major Brooke one of the Commissioners of Maryland to confer with Sir William Berkeley, Governor of Virginia, and William Drummond, Governor of the Southward Plantations, or Commissioners representing them, to prohibit, on account of over-

[23] *Archives of Maryland: Proceedings of the Council of Maryland, 1636-1667.* Baltimore, 1885, page 402.

[24] *Ib.*, page 424.

[25] *Archives of Maryland: Proceedings and Acts of the General Assembly of Maryland, 1637-1664.* Baltimore, 1883, page 460.

[26] *Archives of Maryland: Proceedings of the Council of Maryland, 1636-1667.* Baltimore, 1885, page 541.

production, the planting of tobacco from February 1st, 1666, to February 1st, 1667.[27]   In February, 1667, he took part in an expedition against the Indians.   In 1673 he was still a Burgess for Calvert County.[28]   Major Brooke died in 1676.[29]   His wife was Eleanor, daughter of Richard and Margaret Hatton, and niece of Secretary Thomas Hatton of Maryland.

The eldest son of Major Brooke and his wife, Eleanor Hatton, was Colonel Thomas Brooke of Brookfield, Prince George County, Maryland.   He was Justice of the Calvert County Court in 1684, and from 1689 to 1692, and was Deputy-Commissary for the county in 1686.   In 1697 he was one of the Commissioners to treat with the Piscataway Indians.[30]   He was sworn a Justice of the Provincial Court May 1st, 1694, and was appointed Commissary-General June 5th, 1700.[31]   On June 26th, 1702, he was named Judge of the High Court of Admiralty.   From April, 1692, to 1707 and again from 1715 to 1724 he was a mem-

[27] *Archives of Maryland: Proceedings and Acts of the General Assembly of Maryland, 1666–1676.*   Baltimore, 1884, page 143.

[28] *Ib.*, pages 239, 422.

[29] His will was drawn Oct. 25th, 1676, and proved Dec. 29th, 1676. *Will-Book Liber A—1676, 1677,* folio 123.

Communicated by Mrs. Jane Baldwin, of Annapolis, Maryland.

[30] *Liber H. D.,* No. 2, folio 525, Maryland Historical Society, Baltimore.

[31] *Testamentary Proceedings of Prerogative Court* for last note. *Liber XVIII. B, folio 1,* Register of Wills, Annapolis.

ber of the Council of Maryland.[32] In 1720 he was President of the Council and Acting-Governor of the Province. He died in 1730.[33] As Deputy Governor, Colonel Brooke wrote the following letter to the Bishop of London :

"MARYLAND, 18th July, 1720.

"My LORD,

"The Government here being in me at present under the Lord Proprietor, I take it to be my indisputable duty to do all I can to promote the true interest of the Church of England established in this Province, as well as I am firmly attached to it by my judgment and inclination.

"I with great pleasure congratulate your Lordship on the happy prospect we have (by the good conduct and example of your Commissary, the Rev^d Mr. Henderson) of putting an end to the unhappy disputes that were on purpose raised among the Clergy about matters that no way concerned their duty (viz'), endeavours to misrepresent our Lord Proprietor. And I can with great truth say that no noblemen can do

---

[32] *Archives of Maryland: Proceedings of the Council of Maryland, 1687,8–1693.* Baltimore, 1890, pages 271-555, *passim. Proceedings and Acts of the General Assembly of Maryland, 1684–1692.* Baltimore, 1894, pages 253-360, *passim.*

[33] Colonel Thomas Brooke's will was proved January 25th, 1731. *Will-Book C. C., No. 3, 1730–1734, folio 125 :* Office of Register of Wills, Annapolis, Md.

more than his Lordship has done to convince us all of his regard and zeal for the Protestant religion and Interest.

"As this is an happy prospect, and promises me much ease and satisfaction so long as I shall have the honor of governing, so I humbly pray your Lordship's assistance to perfect so good beginnings by your paternal Injunctions to the Clergy to promote and forward them. They shall never want what service I can do them, nor shall I omit any opportunity to demonstrate that

"I am, my Lord, &c.,

"THOS BROOKE."[34]

Colonel Brooke married first Anne ———, who joined him in a deed dated Feb. 23rd, 1687.

They had

    1. Thomas Brooke, who married Lucy Smith.

    2. Eleanor Brooke, who married first John Tasker, and second Charles Sewall.

    3. Sarah Brooke, who married Philip Lee.

Colonel Brooke married second Barbara (born in 1676 and died in 1754)[35], youngest daughter of

---

[34] William Stevens Perry's *American Colonial Church, Vol. IV., Mary-land*, page 125. Privately printed, 1878. See also pages 121, 122.

[35] The will of Barbara Brooke, widow, was drawn Feb. 4th, 1748-9, and sworn to January 26th, 1754. *Record of Wills, No. 1, folio 470*, Prince George County, Md.

Thomas Dent, of St. Mary's County, and Rebecca[36] his wife, daughter of the Rev. William Wilkinson. Thomas Brooke and Barbara Dent were married before January 4th, 1699–1700, for on that date she joins him in a deed.[37]

Colonel Brooke and Barbara Dent, his second wife, had issue, but the order of birth is not certain, the following children :[38]

Thomas Brooke.
Nathaniel Brooke.
John Brooke.
Benjamin Brooke.
Baker Brooke.
Mary Brooke, who married Dr. Patrick Sim, of Prince George County.
Rebecca Brooke, who married John Howard of Charles County.
Priscilla Brooke, who married Thomas Gantt.
Jane Brooke, who married Alexander Contee.
Elizabeth Brooke, who married Colonel George Beall.
Lucy Brooke, who married Thomas Hodgkin.

[36]Thomas Dent died in 1676; Rebecca, his widow, married secondly Mr. John Adison, also mentioned as *Colonel* John Adison, of Charles and St. Mary's Counties, as his property was in both counties. On October 19th, 1677, she was cited to account for her execution of the estate of her late husband, Thomas Dent, and craved time until her husband, Colonel John Adison, returned to the province; this request was granted. (*Testamentary Proceedings, No. IX., folio 374,* Annapolis.)
Communicated by Mrs. Jane Baldwin, Annapolis, Maryland.

[37]*Liber A, folio 210.* Records of Prince George County, Md. She also joined him in a deed November 6th, 1730. *Liber Q, folio 124,* Records of Prince George County.

[38]The names of the children of Colonel and Mrs. Brooke were communicated by Mrs. Jane Baldwin of Annapolis, Md.

Elizabeth Brooke, daughter of Colonel Thomas Brooke and Barbara Dent, his second wife, married Colonel George Beall[39] of Prince George County, the youngest of the twelve children of Colonel Ninian Beall.

Colonel Ninian Beall was born in 1625,[40] in Scotland, probably either in Fifeshire or Dumbartonshire.

---

[39] "At the request of Mary Beall the following Deed of Gift was Recorded April 2d Anno Domini 1751—

"Maryland SS.   Prince Georges County To all Christian People to whom these presents shall come I Barbara Brooke of the same County and Province afd. send Greeting.   Know ye that I the said Barbara Brooke for and in Consideration of the Natural Love and Affection which I have and do bear to my Grand Daughter Mary Beall (Daughter of Elizabeth & George Beall my son in Law) as well as Five shillings Current money in hand paid as for Divers other good Causes and Considerations me thereunto more Especially moving hath Given and Granted by these Presents doth Give Grant and confirm unto my said Grand Daughter Mary Beall one Negroe Girl named Rebeccah and her Increase To her the said Mary Beall and her heirs for ever.   To have and To hold the afd Negroe Girl and her Increase to my said Grand Daughter Mary Beall and the Heirs of her Body Lawfully Begotten.   But if my said Grand Daughter Mary Beall should Die before she comes of Age or have Lawfull Issue then I do Give Grant and Confirm the Beforementioned Negroe Girl and her Increase To my Grand son Thomas Brooke Beall, and to the Heirs of his Body Lawfully Begotten but in case of Default of such Issue I do Give and Grant the afd Negroe Girl and her Increase to my Grand son Patrick Beall and the Heirs of his Body Lawfully Begotten for ever. And in Case of Default of such Issue then I do hereby Give and Grant the afd Negroe Girl and her Increase unto the Heirs of me the said Barbara Brooke.   In Witness whereof I have hereunto set my hand and affixed my seal this second day of April Anno Domini 1751.

her
"BARBARA ✕ BROOKE."
mark

Liber C, folio 111, Prince George County Records at Marlboro. Communicated by Mrs. Jane Baldwin of Annapolis.

[40] Chancery Records (1712-1724), page 42, in Maryland Land Office, Annapolis.

He was in the Scottish army which fought against Cromwell at the battle of Dunbar in 1650, where he was taken prisoner and soon after transported to Maryland, where he lived, first in Calvert County and afterwards in Prince George County.[41] Of a strong character, he became in a short time, with his knowledge of arms, a man of importance in the miltiary forces of the province. He was very busy fighting the Indians until the end of his life, rising higher and higher until he became a full Colonel.[42]

[41] There is a record of him in the Maryland Land Office of the year 1658 (*Liber 5 Folio* 416). By the family and in Georgetown the name Beall, is pronounced as if it were spelt "bell." Although the scribes at Annapolis spelt Ninian Beall's name in many ways, his descendants now all spell the name, "Beall." He and his family should not be confounded with the following seven emigrants and their descendants:

					Liber.	*Folio.*
Beal,	John,	transported			1658	D.	211
Beale,	"	"			1658	12	551
"	Susan,	"			1676	15	359
"	Thomas,	"			1666	9	436
"	"	of St. Mary's, Service			1672	17	57
"	William,	transported			1664	6	296
"	"	"			1671	16	400

[42] At a meeting of the Governor and Council on May 20th, 1692, the following letter was read:

"May the 19th 1692 Western Branch.
"May it Please your Excellency
"I have here sent you the news inclosed that came to me, I am Just now going up, and will be as Carefull as I can till further Order from your Honour and Council I do intend to keep out Ranging back of the Plantations till further Orders in hast I remain

"To his Excellency the Capt Genl
& Chief Governor in and over
the Province of Maryland.

Your Excellencys Servant to
Command whilst I am
"NINIAN BEALE."

The enclosure spoken of in the above letter referred to an Indian attack. *Archives of Maryland: Proceedings and Acts of the General Assembly of Maryland, 1684-1692.* Baltimore, 1894, page 282.

On July 22d, 1699, the Maryland Assembly passed the following act in recognition of his services:

"An Act of Gratitude to Col. Ninian Beall. *Lib.* L L. No. 2. fol. p. 228. PR.

"Viz. For his Services upon all Incursions and Disturbances of the Neighboring *Indians*, 75 l. Sterling, to be laid out for 3 serviceable Negroes, to him and to his Wife during their Lives, and afterwards to their Children. The said Negroes and their Increase not to be subject to any Executions or Judgments during the Life of Mr. Beall, or his Wife."[43]

He became the owner of many tracts of land, some of rather large extent. In 1703 he received the following grant from Lord Baltimore, which included much of the ground upon which Georgetown now stands:

"Ninian Beales Patt 795 acres Rock of Dumbarton[44]

"Cert *Lib.* D. D.

"Charles absolute Lord and propry of the Province of Maryland, To all etc., know yee that for and in Consederation that Ninian Beale of Prince Georges County hath due unto him seven hundred and ninety

---

[43] *Laws of Maryland at large, 1637-1763*, Annapolis; printed by Jonas Green, Printer to the Province, 1765. Chapter XX.

[44] *Liber C. D., folio 121.* Maryland Land Office at Annapolis.

five acres of land within our said Province being due
unto him by virtue of a warrant for five hundred
acres, granted him the nineteenth day of May, one
thousand seven hundred and two and another warrant
for nine hundred and twenty acres granted him the
sixth day of May, one thousand seven hundred and
two as appears in our Land office and upon such
Conditions and terms as are expressed in our Conditions of Plantacons of our said Province bearing
date the fifth day of April one thousand six hundred
eighty and four and remaining upon record in our
said province together with such alteracons as in them
are made by our further Condicons bearing date the
fourth day of December one thousand six hundred
ninety and six and registered in our land office of
our said province, Wee doe therefore hereby grant
unto him the said Ninian Beale all that Tract or
parcell of land called Rock of Dumbarton lying in
the said County Beginning at the South last corner
Tree, of a Tract of land taken for Robert Mason
standing by Potomeck River side at the mouth of
Rock Creek on a point running thence with the said
land North North West, six hundred and forty ps.
thence last three hundred and twenty ps. then South
six deg: and a half Easterly four hundred ps. then
with the straight line by the Creek and River to the

first bound.   Containing and then laid out for seven
hundred ninety and five acres, more or less according
to the Cert. thereof of Survey taken and returned
into our land Office bearing date the fourth day of
November one thousand seven hundred and two and
there remaining together with all rights profits bene-
fits and priveledges thereunto belonging Royall mines
excepted To have and to hold the same unto him the
said Ninian Beale his heirs and assigns forever to be
holden of us and our heirs as of our mannor of
Calverton in free and Common Soccage by fealty
only for all manner of Services yielding and paying
therefore yearly unto us and our heirs at our receipt
at the City of S'Maries at the two most usuall feasts
in the year Viz. at the feast of the Annuncacon of the
blessed Virgin Mary and S'Michaell the archangell.
by even and equal porcons the rent of one pound
eleven shill^s. and nine pence half penny Ster: in
silver or gold and for a fine upon every alienacon of
the said land or any part or parcell thereof one whole
year rent in silver or gold or the full value thereof in
such Commodities as wee and our heirs or such
Officer as shall be appointed by us and our heirs
from time to time to Collect and receive the same
shall accept in discharge thereof at the choice of us
and our heirs or such officer or officers as aforesd

provided that if the paid sume for a fine for alienation shall not be paid to us and our heirs or such officer or Officers as afore said before such alienacon and the said alienacon entred upon Record either in the provinciall Court or in the County Court where the same parcell of land lyeth within one month next after such alienacon the said alienacon shall be void of no effect Given under our greater seale at arms, this eighteenth day of November, one thousand seven hundred and three. Witness our Trusty and well beloved Coll Henry Darnall keeper of our said greater seale in our said Province of Maryland."[45]

Ninian Beall's will, which is on record at Annapolis, is as follows:

"In the Name of God Amen.

"I Ninian Beall of Prince Georges County in the Province of Maryland being indisposed in Body but of sound and perfect memory God be praised for the same and considering the Mortality of humane, Nature and uncertainty of life doe make ordain constitute and appoint this to be my last Will and Testament in manner and forme following Viz[t]

---

[45] The Calverts made many other grants to Ninian Beall ; for instance, " Bellfast " in Calvert County was a grant September 13th, 1683, to "Captain Ninian Beale" by "Charles Absolute Lord and Propty. of the Province of Maryland and Avalon Lord Baron of Baltimore etc." *Liber S. D., No. A, folio 1.* Maryland Land Office, Annapolis.

"Impris, I give and bequeath my soul into the hands of Almighty God in hopes of free pardon for all my sins and as for my Body to be committed to the Earth from whence it came to be decently buried at the Discretion of my trustees hereafter mentioned.

"Item I will and bequeath that, all my Debts and funeral charges be first paid and satisfyed and as for what portion of my worldly goods as shall be then remaining I bequeath and bestow the same in manner following.

"Item. I doe give and bequeath unto my son George my plantation and Tract of land called the Rock of Dunbarton lying and being at Rock Creek and containing four hundred and eighty acres with all the stock thereon both cattle and Hoggs them and their, increase unto my said son George and unto his heirs for ever.

"Item, I doe give and bequeath unto my said son George Beall his choice of one of my feather beds bolster and Pillow and other furniture thereunto belonging with two Cows and calves and half my sheep from off this plantation, I now live on unto him and his heirs for ever.

"Item, I doe give and bequeath unto my son in Law Andrew Hambleton my negro woman Alic unto him and his heirs for ever.

"Item, I give and bequeath unto my Granddaughter Mary Beall the daughter of my son Ninian Beall deceased the one half part of all my moveables or personal estate as Cattle and Hogs Horses Household goods after my Legacyes before bequeathed are paid and satisfied unto her the said Mary and to her heirs for ever.

"Item   I give and bequeath unto my said Granddaughter Mary Beall all that part of Bacon Hall that lyeth on the south side of the road that goeth to Mount Calvert to her the said Mary and unto her heirs for ever.

"Item   I give and bequeath to my Grandson Samuel Beall all the remainder part of Bacon Hall together with the Plantation and Orchyard and tobacco houses thereunto belonging (with this proviso) that when he comes to the age of one and twenty that he make over by a firm conveyance all his, right and title that he hath unto a certain Tract of land called Sanes [or Sams] Beginning on the south side of the said road goeing to Mount Calvert unto the said Mary and unto her heirs for ever but if my said Grandson should happen to dye before he arrive to be of that age to make over the land soe as aforesaid then I do give & bequeath unto my said Granddaughter Mary the whole Tract of Bacon Hall with the houses and Orchyard thereon unto her and her heirs for ever.

"Item   I give and bequeath unto my s^d Grandson Samuel Beall my Water Mill Lying upon Collington Branch with the stones Iron work houses and all other Mattercalls, thereunto belonging unto the said Samuel and unto his heirs for ever.

"Item   I give and bequeath unto my Son in Law Joseph Belt[46] part of a tract of land called Good Luck containing two hundred forty five acres he allowing unto my heirs the sum of four thousand pounds of tobacco according to our former agreement he deducting what I doe owe him on his books for severall wares and merchandizes had of him to the said Joseph and unto his heirs for

"Item   that whereas I owe several debts I doe empower my trustees hereafter named to enable them to pay the same to sell a certain Tract of land called the Recovery lying and being in the freshes of Patuxent River near the head of the Western Branch to be sold it containing four hundred acres, the aforesaid tract of land bequeathed unto my son Belt is adjoining there unto

"Item   I doe give and bequeath unto my son Charles Beall a Book of Bishop Coopers work the acts of the Church and the Chronicles of King Charles the first and King Charles the second, and I doe

---

[46] Miss Catherine Dulany Belt says his wife was Margery Beall.

request and oblige my son Charles my Bell and my
son George to son to send for a Dozen of books
entitled an advise to young and old and middle age
set forth by one Mr Christopher Ness. the books to
be distributed among my Grand children and God
sons.

"Item   I give and bequeath unto my son Charles
a thousand acres of land called Dunn Back lying on
the South side of great Choptank in a Creek called
Wattses Creek unto him and his heirs forever

"And lastly I do make ordain Declare and appoint
my Grandson Samuel Bell to be my sole and whole
Executor of this my last will & testament and I doe
devise my loving son Charles Bell Joseph Belt and
George Bell to doe and perform my devise as above
exprest and to act & doe for my executor until he
shall arrive to the age of one and twenty hereby
revoking and annulling all former and other wills by
me at any time heretofore made and signed.   And
doe desire my said sons to use their best care and
endeavour that my two Grand Children the Children
of my beloved son Ninian Beall deceased to be
brought up and have that education suitable to their
estate, I doe also appoint my said sons Trustees to
this my will to make their appearance every Easter
Tuesday or any other time as they shall think a

more fitting time at my dwelling plantation yearly
to inspect into all affairs thereof and of a yearly
increase of all the Creatures upon my plantation
and at the Mill for and on the behalf of my two Grand
Children who are to be joint Sharers therein my Granddaughter to have her part at the day of her Marriage.

"In testimony whereof I have to this my last will
and testament set my hand & seal this fifteenth day
of January in the year of our Lord God one thousand
seven hundred and seventeen.

The mark of

"NINIAN × BEALL.   [SEAL]"[47]

Though Ninian Beall made his mark to his will,
he was a man of education for those days, since he
signed his name often, as is shown by the records at
Annapolis.   He died in the year 1717 in his ninety-
third year.

[47] *Liber W. B. No. 6, folio 504 + c.*   Register of Wills for Anne
Arundel County, Maryland.

There are on record at Marlboro, Prince George County, Md., a
number of deeds of gift from "Coll. Ninian Beall And Ruth his Wife,"
dated March 10th, 1706.   These deeds mention their sons Charles,
Ninian Jr., Thomas, John and George, and their daughters Hester, Mary
and Rechell.   *Liber C, folio 185, 186.*

James Moore in a deposition, August 16th, 1708, speaks of Colonel
Ninian Beall as his brother. *Liber P. C. 2. Chancery Records* (1671-1712)
page 626, Annapolis, Md.   Mrs. Henry Irvine Keyser of Baltimore, a
descendant of Colonel Beall, tells me that it is understood in her family
that Ninian Beall's wife was a Miss Moore.

Colonel George Beall[48] (see page 22) the youngest child of Colonel Ninian Beall, was born at Upper Marlboro,[49] in Prince George County in 1695 and died at Georgetown, D. C., March 15th, 1780. The inscription on his tombstone was as follows :

" Here lieth Colonel George Beall
who departed this Life March 15th
1780 Aged 85 years."

By an act of May 15th, 1751, the Legislature of Maryland provided for laying out a town on the Potomac River, above Rock Creek. For this purpose part of George Beall's land was taken, as well as part of that belonging to a Mr. Gordon. When, in spite of their refusal to sell, the land so taken was divided into lots, Colonel Beall and Mr. Gordon were allowed the privilege of first selecting two lots each as compensation for their lands. After a week's reflection, George Beall sent the following answer :

" If I must part with my property by force, I had better save a little than be totally demolished. Rather than have none, I accept these lots,—Nos. 72 and 79—

---

[48] Among depositions taken in June 1770 concerning a tract of land in Prince George County, the following appears :

" The deposition of Coll. George Beall, aged about Seventy-five years, being first sworn on the Holy Evangels, Deposeth," etc. *Liber A. A., No. 2, folio 206*, Land Records of Prince George County, Md.

[49] Beall family Bible.

said to be Mr. Henderson's and Mr. Edmonston's. But I do hereby protest, and declare that my acceptance of the said lots, which is by force, shall not debar me from future redress from the Commissioners or others, if I can have the rights of a British subject. God save King George!

"GEORGE BEALL.

"MARCH 7, 1752."[50]

He built, what was for those days, a fine, large, brick house which still stands on the present N Street, near Thirty-first Street.[51]   He was buried along side of his wife (see page 22) in the family burying ground near their house. The inscription on her tombstone was as follows:

"Here lieth the Body of Elizabeth Beall the wife of Colonel George Beall who departed this Life October the 2nd: 1748 Aged about 49 years."

In recent years their bodies, with those of their children, were removed to Oak Hill. It is held by many of the inhabitants of Georgetown, that Georgetown was named after Colonel George Beall. On January 18th, 1720, he received a grant of thirteen

[50] *The Chronicles of Georgetown, D. C., from 1751 to 1878*, by Richard P. Jackson of the Washington Bar. Washington, D. C.; R. O. Polkinhorn, 1878, pages 3-5.

[51] It may be that this house was built by his son, Thomas Beall.

hundred and eighty acres known as " the Addition to the Rock of Dumbarton."[52]   His will was probated at Rockville, Montgomery County, Maryland, and is as follows :

"In the name of God Amen, I George Beall of Montgomery County and State of Maryland, being weak of Body but of perfect mind and disposing memory, and bearing in mind the certainty of Death, and uncertainty of life, do ordain this to be my last Will & Testament, Renouncing & Disanuling all former Wills, and first I Will my Soul to God in whose mercy with the merits of Jesus Christ I depend for Salvation, Secondly, that my Body be Buried in a decent and Christian like manner—And thirdly, I will that all my Just debts be paid out of the Estate it hath pleased God to bless me with, & the Remainder to be Divided in manner and form following, Vizt,—

"Item, I give and bequeath to my son George Beall   [The will is effaced at this point.]

"Item, I give all my houses, and lots in Georgetown to my son Thomas Beall and also all that tract or parcel of land called Cunjurors Disappointment and also part of Dumbarton, to be Divided by the great branch that leads to the Saw Mill thence to the

---

[52] *Liber J. L., No. A., folio 55*, Maryland Land Office, Annapolis.

Main Road, all that part that lies to the southward to belong to my G. son Thomas Beall

"Item, I give unto my Daughter Elizabeth Evans my Negro fellow Jack, to serve four years and then to be set free—

"Signed Sealed and Acknowledged to be my last Will & testament in presents of us this 15th day of March 1780.

"GEO BEALL   [SEAL]

"W. SMITH
   RICHARD CHENEY
   ABRAᴹ BOYD."

Colonel and Mrs. Beall had twelve children as follows :[53]

> Esther, d. y.
> Thomas, d. aged seventeen years.
> Mary, d. aged sixteen years.
> George, b. in 1729.
> Levin, d. in Martinique.
> Patrick.
> Thomas (2nd) d. y.
> Rebeckah.
> Lucy Magruder.
> Elizabeth Evans.
> Mary (2nd)
> Thomas (3rd) born in 1748 (see page 57).

[53]From the family Bible that belonged to George C. Washington; communicated by Mrs. Henry Irvine Keyser, of Baltimore.

George, the fourth child and second son of Colonel George Beall[54] and Elizabeth Brooke his wife, was also in the army as the inscription on his tombstone shows:

" Sacred to the Memory of Colonel George Beall. He was born in George Town on the 26th day of February 1729.   He died October 15th 1807 in the

---

[54] A grandson of the second Colonel George Beall, the Rev. Thomas Bloomer Balch, speaks thus in his *Reminiscences of Georgetown* of some of the Beall family :

" George Beall, the son of Ninian [Beall] was the immediate progenitor of George and Thomas Beall, who were respectable inhabitants of Georgetown.   Ninian [Beall] being a friend of the Hanoverian succession, probably gave name to his son from this fact.   George, of George, died in 1807, and was buried in the family cemetery, which is nearly opposite to the house now occupied by Dr. Riley.

*   *   *   *   *   *   *   *

" He married a Magruder.   The clan of the McGregors had been rather turbulent in the highlands of Scotland, but the Magruders behaved very well after their removal to Maryland, about the middle of the seventeenth century.

*   *   *   *   *   *   *   *

" It is unnecessary to say anything about the descendants of Colonel George Beall [1729–1807] except in connection with our town.   His son, Thomas Brooke [Beall] was at one time President of the Farmers and Mechanics' Bank, and died in 1820.   In 1781, his eldest daughter [Elizabeth Beall] was married to the Rev. Dr. Balch, once pastor of the Presbyterian church on Bridge Street, who is introduced into these reminiscences by special request from many of our citizens.   Thomas Beall, brother of George [the second] made one of the additions to the corporate limits of this town.   Seventy-five years ago he built a house on the heights called Dumbarton, and died in the fall of 1819."

Reminiscences of Georgetown, D. C.   Second Lecture delivered March 9th, 1859, by Rev. T. B. Balch.   Washington ; Henry Polkinhorn, 1859, page 7.

79th Year of his Age.   He lived respected and died lamented."[55]

His will, which is on record in Washington, D. C., is as follows :

"In the name of God Amen I George Beall of Washington County in the State of Columbia, being in perfect health and of a sound and disposing mind and memory, do make and ordain this my last will and testament, first revoking all other wills. It is my will and desire that all my just debts be paid.   Item, I give and bequeath unto my beloved wife Elizabeth Beall all the real and personal property that I have received by her with their increase. Likewise, I give her negro Bill and a mullattow girl named Sela and my cochehee with two horses that is fitting for a carriage and one hundred dollars to buy a morning (moung) ring, but she is to have no rite of dowry to any part of my estate, if she should want to retake any part or parsell of my estate or my will then all what I have received by her to be

---

[55] In the *Archives of Maryland: Journal and Correspondence of the Maryland Council of Safety*, July 7th–December 31st, 1776 (Baltimore, 1893), at page 293, it is recorded that "Captⁿ George Beall" was appointed September 21st, 1776, inspector of "George Town Warehouse, in the Lower district of Frederick County."   And in the *Journal and Correspondence of the Council of Safety*, January 1st–March 20th, 1777, and the *Journal and Correspondence of the State Council*, March 20th, 1777–March 28th, 1778 (*Archives of Maryland*, Baltimore, 1897), a Major George Beall is twice mentioned, pages 296 and 373.

brought into my apprasement both real and personal. After my wife's decease Bill and Sela to be
devided between my children and Sela's increase if
any. Item, I give and devise unto my eldest son
George Beall one hundred dollars. I also give and
bequeave unto the children of the said George Beall
the negroe named in a bill of sale from him to me
recorded in Montgomery County Court with all that
increase but not till after the death of the said
George Beall and his wife. I likewise give and bequeath to George Beall two children Patrick Beall
and Ann Beall three small negroes apiece with the
one that each has got a piece. I likewise give the
said George Beall an equal part of my household furniture and an equal part of all my stock. Item, I
give and bequeath to my son Levin Beall the land he
now lives on during his life and his present wife's
life ; then after their decease to be equally divided betwixt his two children, John and Anna Beall to them
and their heirs for ever. I likewise give and bequeath to John Beall and Anna Beall all the negroes
that Levin C. Beall has in his possition to be equally
divided between John and Anna Beall after their
father and mother's decease. I likewise give the said
John and Anna Beall each of them three small negroes apiece such as my executors shall think proper.

I likewise give Levin C. Beall one hundred dollars and an equal part of my household furniture with an equal part of the stock. Item, I give and bequeave to my grandson Thomas Beall of Eras. Beall three negroes such as my executors shall think proper and four hundred dollars, to be taken out of my houses and lotts. Item, I make and do ordain my two sons Hezk. Beall and Capt. Thos. B. Beall my whole executors and administrators jointly and severally on all my estate. I give and bequeath to my two sons Hezh. Beall and Capt. Thos. B. Beall the grave yard lott to begin at the end of my two lotts that lays in front of the street and to run to a lott known by the name of Mrs. White's and then with said lott north or thereabouts to the end supposed to be one hundred and twenty feet, then to run about west, so as to make it square in the garding, and then to run about south with a straight line to the beginning of the first line, to them and their heirs, executors, administrators or assigns for ever. Item, I give and bequeave to my son Hezekiah Beall the remainder part of the thousand pounds that I was to give him, likewise the six negroes and their increase that I have given him, likewise an equal share of my stock and household goods. Item, I give and bequeath to my son Capt. Thos. Brooke Beall three negroes that is all to make

up his six negroes with the three that he has gott,
likewise his balance due him of his thousand pounds
and likewise I give him all the land that I hold on
Senaca Creek that I bought of him, he first paying to
the estate six hundred dollars to pay off the legacies—
Likewise an equal part of stock and household furniture. Item I give and bequeath to the Revd.
Stephen B. Balch Nell and Lydia, but their increase
to be equally divided betwixt his children. Whereas
Lydia has three or four children now I give the oldest
child to Lewis P. W. Balch, the next oldest to Geo.
Balch, and the next oldest to Anna Balch and the
next oldest to Harriet Balch and so continue until
they all get equall alike in case the two negro women
should breed ; likewise I give Lewis P. W. Balch one
hundred and fifty dollars out of my estate. I give
and bequeath to Capt. John Rose the six negroes that
he had of me and their increase, and to have his
thousand pounds made up to him as there is a great
proportion already paid ; likewise I give him an equall
part of the stock and household furniture. Item I
give all the rest of my estate, after my just debts is
paid and all these legacies that I have made is taken
out of my houses and lotts in George Town or Thos.
Beall of Geo. addition to Georgetown except the
Grave yard lott which I have given to my two sons

Hezk. Beall and Capt. Thos. B. Beall, it is my desire
that the above property be equally divided betwixt
the following children to wit: Hezk. Beall, Capt.
Thos. B. Beall, Elizabeth Balch and Anna Rose.
Item, it is my desire that my executors and administrators give to George Beall, my eldest son, one
negro at their discression for during his life and his
wife's life and afterwards to be divided between his
two children Patrick Beall and his daughter Ann
Beall. It is also my desire that my executors and administrators give to my son Levin C. Beall one grone
negro at their discression of my executors during his
and his wife's life, and afterwards to be divided between his two children John Beall and Anna Beall.
Of my executors, being subscribed and set down before the signing of this instrument of writing.

In testimony whereof I have hereunto set my hand
and affixed my seal *this* eleventh day of June one
thousand eight hundred and two.

"GEORGE BEALL.

❋   ❋   ❋   ❋   ❋   ❋   ❋

" Proved October 20th, 1807."[56]

He married Elizabeth Magruder (originally Mc-
Gregor). Among their children were Thomas Brooke

[56] *Wills No 1, J. H., folio 137.* Register of Wills, Washington, D. C.

Beall[57] who died in 1820, Elizabeth Beall, and Anna Beall who married in 1792 at Georgetown, "Captain" John Rose. Elizabeth Beall was born in Georgetown in 1762 and died there June 27th, 1827. On July 10th, 1781, she was married by the Rev. Isaac Stockton Keith to the Rev. Stephen Bloomer Balch, then Rector of the Presbyterian Church of Georgetown. The ladies of Georgetown being patriotic, positively refused to drink tea during the progress of the Revolution, and so the cups used at the wedding were not much larger than thimbles.[58] Dr. Balch was the son of James Balch and was born April 5th, 1747, on Deer Creek, Harford County, Maryland. His family came originally from southwestern England—from Somerset and Devon. After graduating at Princeton College in 1774, he went to

[57] The will of Thomas Brooke Beall of Washington, D. C., was signed November 23d, 1808. The last codicil was dated "George Town 9th July 1816." The will was proved at Washington, D. C., October 14th, 1820.

"Item 12. I leave Hezk. Beall or his children one third of my estate, Anna Rose one third or her children and one third to Thomas [Bloomer] Balch, Anna Balch, Eliza Balch and Jane Whann Balch, after all the legacies are paid the balance is to go as I have stated in this Item. The one third that I have left to Mrs. Balch's children is to be equally divided among the above named children. And lastly, I do hereby constitute and appoint Hezk. Beall, Capt. John Rose and Stephen B. Balch to be my executors of this my last will & testament." *Wills No. 3, H. C. H., folio 91*, Register of Wills, Washington, D. C.

[58] *Reminiscences of Georgetown, D. C.* A lecture delivered in Georgetown D. C., January 20th, 1859, by Rev. T. B. Balch. Washington: Henry Polkinhorn, 1859, page 15.

Lower Marlboro, Calvert County, Maryland, where
he took charge of a classical academy. On October
1st, 1775, he was commissioned captain in the Calvert County militia: he held this command for three
years and was in actual service against the enemy
from December 1st, 1775, to December 1st, 1777.[59]
When the British appeared on the shores of the
Patuxent River and Chesapeake Bay, he marched
out with his company to assist in repulsing them.
He was in a number of actions, and though frequently offered promotion, declined it, inasmuch as he
thought he could be of more service on the Chesapeake border, with all of which he was familiar from
childhood, and at the same time could continue his
preparation for the ministry. In 1778 when the feel-
ing was universal that, owing to the defeat of Bur-
goyne (1777) and the French alliance, our independence was secured, and the acknowledgment of it was
merely a question of time, he resigned from the
service in order to give himself up more assiduously
to his clerical duties.

In 1780 he was called by the Presbyterians of
Georgetown on the Potomac to establish a church
among them. Accepting, he arrived there March

[59] *Records of the Revolutionary War*, by W. T. R. Saffell, New York,
1858, page 537.

16th, 1780, and remained in charge of the church he founded, until his death fifty-three years afterwards.

Among his friends were Thomas Jefferson and Albert Gallatin. A few weeks after the death of General Washington, Dr. Balch gave notice that he would speak of the life and services of the departed statesman. He preached in the open air to more than a thousand people, from the last verse of the tenth chapter of the book of Esther, " For Mordecai the Jew, was next unto King Ahasuerus, and great among the Jews, and accepted of the multitude of his brethren, seeking the wealth of his people, and speaking peace to all his seed." He was a firm believer in the rights of the individual and was in favor of gradually liberating the slaves and sending them to Liberia. He had a robust, vigorous constitution and a bold honest countenance. He was a lover of books, and among the classics he preferred Horace to Virgil.

" On Sunday morning, September 22, 1833, at nine o'clock A. M., as he was preparing to go to church to perform his official duties," Mr. Jackson of Georgetown says,[60] "he was stricken with apoplexy and sank to rest like the sun without a cloud to hide his lustre. As the news of his death spread through the town the citizens,

[60] Article on Dr. Balch in the Washington *Evening Star* of April 1st, 1893, by W. S. Jackson, Esq., of Georgetown, D. C.

irrespective of religious creed, expressed themselves
with one accord: 'Well done, good and faithful servant, enter thou into the joy of thy Lord.' A successful
plaster cast of his face was taken just after his death.
On Monday the Board of Aldermen and Common
Council of Georgetown passed the following resolution:

" ' That we have learned with deep regret the death
of our aged and venerable fellow citizen, Doctor
Stephen Bloomer Balch, who for more than fifty-three
years, has been a useful and honored minister of religion in the town, illustrating the holy profession he
made through his long career by a life of uniform
piety towards God, and benevolence, liberality and
kindness to his fellow men, descending to his tomb
full of years, and rich in the reverence, esteem and
love of the whole community.

" ' Resolved, that as a testimony of respect to his
memory, the members and officers of this corporation
will attend his funeral to-morrow (Tuesday) at ten
o'clock A. M.

" ' Resolved, that the clerk of the corporation be re-
quested to transmit a copy of these resolutions to the
family of the deceased.'

" The town was draped in mourning, business places
were closed, and all the bells tolled as the remains of
this faithful apostle of God were carried from his resi-

dence, No. 3302 N Street, to the church where he had
so often performed the last sad rites to hundreds and
thousands.   Ministers of all denominations, including
eight priests, representing the Catholic Church, who
had loved and venerated him in life, joined in the funeral cortege.   When the hearse reached the church
the procession was still forming at the residence.

" The funeral sermon, an eloquent discourse on the
life and services of the deceased, was preached by the
Rev. Elijah Harrison, of Alexandria, Virginia, from
Acts viii. 2 : ' And devout men carried Stephen to his
burial, and made great lamentation over him.'   After
the funeral sermon his remains were incased in the
front wall of the church.

" His life was checkered with many severe trials.
Dug out of one home, flooded out of another and
burnt out of a third, yet his fortitude and piety, resig-
nation and cheerfulness forsook him not.   Keeping
his eye steadfastly fixed on his sacred calling, he was
to his expiring day faithful to his Master.

   *   *   *   *   *   *   *

"In October, 1835, a handsome monument was
erected by his family to his memory in front of the
church he founded and so long presided over.   It was
of white marble, representing a pyramidal tablet rest-
ing upon a solid Ionic base against the wall between

the doors of the main entrance, with no other orna-
ment than a wreath beautifully sculptured at the top.
It bore the following inscription:

'Sacred
To the memory of
Stephen Balch, D. D.
Who died September 22, 1833,
In the eighty-seventh year of his age.
He was the founder of this church,
And for more than half a century
Its revered pastor.
He planted the gospel in this town,
And his example was for many years
A light to its inhabitants.
He being dead, yet speaketh.

'Reliquiae mortales
Stephani Bloomer Balch, D. D.,
Sub hoc marmore
Inhumantur.
His children have erected this tablet
To record
The virtue of the dead and the
Gratitude of the living.'

"In the spring of 1873, when the church was demolished, his remains were reintered in the Presbyterian cemetery on 33rd Street near the chapel.   In the
spring of 1874 the philanthropic William W. Corcoran

wrote to his children requesting the privilege of re-
moving the remains to Oak Hill cemetery. Writing
to his son, the Rev. Thomas B. Balch, he said: 'I
knew your father from boyhood, and the sentiments
of profound esteem with which at an early age I
regarded him were undiminished at the close of his
protracted and exemplary life.' And on June 18,
1874, the remains of this apostle of God were reintered near the Swiss Chapel in Oak Hill cemetery.
A mural tablet ordered by W. W. Corcoran was
mounted on the wall of the Swiss Chapel bearing the
following inscription in letters of gold:

'In honor of
Stephen Bloomer Balch, D. D.,
Born
On "Deer Creek", near Balt., Md.,
April, A. D. 1747,
Came to Georgetown, D. C.,
March 16, A. D. 1780.
Died September 22, A. D. 1833,
He planted the Gospel in
Georgetown. Founded
"The Bridge Street Presbyterian
Church"
And was for more than fifty years
Its Pastor.
In life he Practiced what he Preached.
No Eulogy can add to such
A record.' "

Dr. and Mrs. Balch had eleven children as follows :

1. Ann Amia, d. y.
2. Harriet.
3. Alfred.
4. Lewis P. W.
5. George Beall.
6. Hezekiah James, d. unmarried.
7. Thomas Bloomer.
8. Franklin, d. y.
9. Ann Eleanora.
10. Elizabeth Maria.
11. Jane Whann.

2. Harriet Balch was born at Georgetown, D. C., June 17th, 1783. She married first James R. Wilson, U. S N., and after his death Major-General Alexander Macomb, commander-in-chief of the United States Army, who fought the battle of Plattsburg in 1814.[61] General and Mrs. Macomb lived in Washington in a large house which still stood in 1897 on Farragut Square at the north west corner of Seventeenth and I Streets. Mrs. Macomb died May 22d, 1869.

3. Alfred Balch was born at Georgetown, D. C., September 17th, 1785. He graduated at Princeton College in the class of 1805, and studied for the Bar. In 1813

---

[61] An oil picture of General Macomb that he had painted for his wife, taken after the battle of Plattsburg and now in the writer's possession, shows him standing in full uniform and looking into the distance : his orderly holds his horse close by, and in the background the tents of the American Army are seen.

he went to Nashville, Tennessee, upon legal business. There he remained, and soon gained the friendship of Andrew Jackson, which lasted until the death of the hero of New Orleans. Jackson, when President, named him Commissioner of Indian treaties, and in 1840 Martin Van Buren appointed him United States District Judge for the middle district of Florida.[62] He died at his country place, Rose Mont, near Nashville, on June 21st, 1853. He married twice: first Mary Lewis, and after her death Anna Newman. He had one child, Alfred Newman, who died in 1840.

4. Lewis Penn Witherspoon Balch was born at Georgetown, D. C., on December 31st, 1787. He graduated at Princeton College in 1806, where he was a member of Whig Hall, and then studied law with his kinsman (afterwards Chief Justice) Roger Brooke Taney. His father taught him that slavery ought to disappear, and, accordingly, in 1834, he liberated all his slaves and sent twenty-two of them to Liberia, paying for their passage. In March, 1865, he was chosen a State Circuit Judge for the north eastern

---

[62] "I nominate to the Senate Alfred Balch, of Tennessee, to be judge of the United States for the middle district of Florida, for the term of four years, in place of Thomas Randall, whose term of service has expired.

"M. VAN BUREN.
"WASHINGTON, March 10th, 1840."

Executive Proceedings of the Senate, Vol. IV., page 265.

counties of West Virginia, and served in those troublesome times with credit until the following March. He contributed to the *Southern Literary Messenger* a number of biographical sketches—on Roger Brooke Taney, Daniel Sheffy, Samuel Cooper, Robert White, Lawrence Everheard and others. He died August 29th, 1868. On March 14th, 1811, he married Elizabeth Willis Wever, daughter of John Adam Wever (originally von Weber) of Virginia. She was born May 10th, 1790, and died July 7th, 1874.

Besides several children who died young, Judge and Mrs. Balch had six children who grew up ; they were all born at Leesburg, Loudon County, Virginia.

i. Lewis P. W. Balch, born February 23rd, 1814, studied at West Point and Princeton College and was admitted to the ministry of the Episcopal Church ; he married first Anna Jay, daughter of William Jay of New York, and granddaughter of Chief Justice Jay ; he married secondly Emily Wiggin.

ii. Catherine Balch, born November 28th, 1815.

iii. Virginia Balch, born March 18th, 1818.

iv. Thomas Balch, born July 23d, 1821. He studied two years at Columbia College, and then read law with Stephen Cambreling and was admitted to the Bar. In an open letter, to which Horace Greeley gave a place in the New York *Tribune*, on May 13th, 1865, he was the first to propose that the *Alabama* and other differences then pending between the United States and England should be decided by a Court of Arbitration; from that seed the Geneva Tribunal (1872) grew. From 1859 to 1873 he lived in Europe, residing chiefly at Paris. While there he wrote and published in 1872 an account of the part that the French took in the War of Independence: it was entitled *Les Français en Amérique pendant la Guerre de l'Indépendance des États-Unis, 1777-1783.* In July, 1876, as one of the Congress of Authors, he contributed a biographical sketch of Dr. William Shippen, " the Elder," a member of the Continental Congress. He married at Woodfield, her father's country place in Philadelphia County, Emily Swift, daughter of Joseph Swift and his wife, Eliza Moore Willing, and granddaughter of Samuel Swift and his wife, Mary, daughter of Lieutenant-Colonel Joseph Shippen.[63]

Issue surname Balch :

Elise Willing.

Edwin Swift, A. B., Harvard University, 1878, and member of the Philadelphia Bar.

Joseph Swift, born July 5th, 1860, at Paris, France, and died there July 3d, 1864.

Thomas Willing, A. B., Harvard University, 1890, and member of the Philadelphia Bar.

---

[63] *Letters and Papers relating chiefly to the Provincial History of Pennsylvania, with some notices of the writers,* by Thomas Balch, Philadelphia, 1855, page xciii.

v. Alexandrine Macomb, born September 6th, 1828.

vi. Stephen Fitzhugh, born March 14th, 1831.

5. George Beall Balch was born August 16th. 1789, at Georgetown, D. C.   He was a planter at Moulton, Alabama, and died June 2d, 1831.   He married his cousin, Martha Rogers Balch.

With others who died young, they had

George Beall Balch.   He was born January 3d, 1821, at Shelbyville, Tennessee.   He entered the Naval Academy.   He was in the Mexican war and took part in the first attack on Alvarado, November 1st, 1846, and he was a midshipman with Perry in Japan. During the Civil War he commanded the U. S. S. *Pawnee* of the Atlantic coast blockading squadron. In 1878 he became Rear Admiral and was in command at the Naval Academy at Annapolis from 1879 to 1881 and then commanded the Pacific squadron until he was retired in 1883, having reached the limit of age for active service.   He married first Julia Grace Vinsen.

Issue surname Balch :
  George Vinsen.
  Stephen Bloomer.
  Julia Grace.
  Margaret Cassandier.
  Harriet Ann.

Admiral Balch married second, Mary Ellen Booth, daughter of James Booth, Chief Justice of Delaware.

Issue surname Balch :
  Mary Ellen.
  Alfred.
  Anna.
  Francis DuPont.
  Amy Rogers.

6. Hezekiah James Balch, was born April 16th, 1791, at Georgetown, D. C., and died unmarried March 17th, 1821.[64]

7. Thomas Bloomer Balch was born February 28th, 1793, at Georgetown, D. C. He graduated at Princeton in 1813 and was a Presbyterian clergyman of much note. He received an honorary Doctor's degree from his *alma mater*. For several years he was assistant to his father in the church at Georgetown, and then he accepted a call to the church at Snow Hill, Maryland. He frequently wrote for the *Southern Literary Messenger*, and published "Christianity and Literature," 1826, "The Ringwood Discourses," 1850, etc. He

---

[64] He was named after his uncle, the Rev. Hezekiah James Balch, who was born on Deer Creek, Harford County, Maryland, in 1746, graduated at Princeton in 1766, was a minister of the Presbyterian Church, went in 1769 to Macklenburg County, North Carolina, where in 1775 he took a leading part in the Mecklenburg Declaration of Independence, and died unmarried early in 1776. Many chroniclers have confused the Rev. H. J. Balch with his brother the Rev. James Balch, who was born on Deer Creek, December 25th, 1750, and settled in the West ; and also with their cousin the Rev. Hezekiah Balch, who was born in Harford County, Maryland, in 1741, graduated at Princeton in 1766, and settled in Tennessee, where he founded and became the first President of Greenville College.

was very fond of geography, took a great interest in Liberia, and was an active member of the Colonization Society. He died February 14th, 1878, at "Macomb Manse," near Greenwich, Virginia. He married Susan Carter, daughter of Charles Beale Carter of "Shirley" on the James River, who was a half uncle of General Robert E. Lee, C. S. A.; Charles Beale Carter married his first cousin, Anne Beale Carter, also a cousin of General Lee. Dr. and Mrs. Balch had eleven children.

Issue surname Balch:

1. Annie Carter.
2. Elizabeth Macomb.
3. Robert Monroe, Lieutenant-Colonel in the C. S. A.; he was in the Western Army, and at the fight at Fort Donelson had his horse shot under him, but mounted another.[65]
4. Charles Carter, Captain in the C. S. A.; he was at the battle of Fort Donelson.
5. Harriet, d. y.
6. Chalmas Page.
7. Leimaeus.
8. William Cowper ⎱ twins
9. Felyx Neff ⎰
10. Mary Landon.
11. Julia Ringwood.

9. Anna Eleanora Balch was born at Georgetown, D. C., August 14th, 1799. She married Captain James C. Wilson.

---

[65] "Balch's (R. M.) Cavalry. See Tennessee Troops, Confederate, 18th Battalion." *Miscellaneous Documents of the House of Representatives for the 2d session of the 49th Congress,* vol. II., page 904.

10. Elizabeth Maria Balch was born at Georgetown, D. C., April 15th, 1802. She married the Rev. Septinis Tustin, of the Presbyterian Church, at one time Chaplain of the United States Senate.

11. Jane Whann Balch was born at Georgetown. D. C., February 14th, 1805, and died March 5th, 1884. She married William Williamson.

Thomas Beall, known always as "of George," (see page 36) was born September 27th, 1748, and died October 5th, 1819. He married September 26th, 1773, Nancy or Ann, daughter of John Orme, and granddaughter of the Rev. John Orme and Ruth Edmonson of Wiltshire, England. Ann Orme was born July 29th, 1752, and died April 9th, 1827.[66]

They had

    Eliza Ridgely Beall.

    Harriett Ann Beall, who was born February 15th, 1791, and married August 5th, 1808, John Peter.

Eliza Ridgely Beall was born November 22nd, 1786, and died July 1st, 1820. She married September 1st,

Communicated by Mrs. Henry Irvine Keyser.

1807, Colonel George Corbin Washington, son of William Augustine Washington and his cousin, Jane Washington, his wife. William Augustine Washington was the son of General Washington's older half-brother, Augustine Washington, who married Anne Aylett, while Jane Washington was the daughter of General Washington's brother, John Augustine Washington, who married Hannah Bushrod. Colonel Washington was born August 20th, 1789, at Haywood, Westmoreland County, Virginia, and died July 7th, 1854, at Georgetown, D. C. He represented the Montgomery County district of Maryland in the 20th, 21st, and 22d Congresses.

Besides several children who died young, Colonel and Mrs. Washington had Lewis William Washington. He was born November 30th, 1812, at Georgetown, D. C., and died at Beall-Air, Jefferson County, Virginia, October 1st, 1871. On May 17th, 1836, he married Mary Ann Barroll of Baltimore, who was born October 19th, 1817, and died November 16th, 1844.

Issue :

1st. George Corbin Washington, born March, 1837, and died September 30th, 1843.

2d. James Barroll Washington, born August 26th, 1839 and married Mrs. Jane Bretney Lanier Cabell. Have issue.

3d. Mary Ann Washington married November 17th, 1864, to Henry Irvine Keyser of Baltimore, son of Samuel Stouffer Keyser and Elizabeth Wyman, his wife.

Issue surname Keyser:

I. Henry Barroll, married June 1st, 1892, to Caroline Fischer. They have two children, Ann Franklin and Henry Irvine.

II. Samuel Irvine, died young.

III. Lewis Washington, died young.

IV. Irvine.

V. Mary Washington, married June 1st, 1897, to John Stewart, Jr.

VI. William Williams, died young.

4th. Eliza Ridgely Beall Washington, married April 25th, 1865, E. Glenn Perine. Have issue.

Lewis William Washington (see page 58) married second, November 6th, 1860, Ella More Basset: they had issue Betty Lewis Washington and William de Hertburn Washington.

Robert Brooke, the emigrant married for his second wife on May 11th, 1635, Mary Mainwaring (see page 10). She came to Maryland with her husband and died in the Province in 1663. She was the daughter of Roger Mainwaring, Bishop of St. David's[67] and

---

[67] Arms of Mainwaring of Cheshire. Argent, two bars, gules.

his wife Cicelia Proper.   He received the degree of
B. A. at All Soul's College, Oxford, February 1607–8,
that of M. A. July 5th, 1611, and those of B. D. and
D. D. July 2d, 1625.   He died at Caermarthen July
1st, 1653.   Walker, in his *Sufferings of the Clergy*,[6]
says of him: "He was born at Stretton in *Shropshire*
(*Though of* a Cheshire *Family;* which Lloyd *saith was
a* Noble *one*), and educated in the University of
Oxford.   He was sometime *Vicar* of *St. Giles's* in
the Fields and *Chaplain* to King *Charles I.* Before
whome preaching (July 27) those *Sermons* which he
Afterwards *Published* and Entituled, *Religion and
Allegiance;* he was called in question for it by the
Parliament, Charged with Endeavouring to *Destroy
the King and Kingdom* by his *Divinity* and *Censured
to be Imprisoned;* was Fined 1000£ and ordered to
make his Submission, and was Disabled to *Have* or
Enjoy any *Preferment* or *Office*.   However, the King
soon after *Pardoned* him, and gave him the Rich
Living of *Stanford-Rivers* in Essex, in 1633 made
him *Dean of Worcester,* and Two Years after Nominated him to this Bishoprick.

*   *   *   *   *   *   *

[6] An Attempt towards recovering an account of the Numbers and
Sufferings of the Clergy of the Church of England * * * * in the
late Times of the Grand Rebellion: By John Walker, M. A.   London
1714, page 76.

'*For the two last Years of his Life, not a week passed without a Message or an Inquiry;* which *he desired God not to remember against his Adversaries,* and adjured all his Friends to Forget." He died at Caermarthen on July 16th, 1653.

Of the sons of Robert Brooke and his second wife, Mary Mainwaring, Roger Brooke was born at Bretnock College, England, on April 8th, 1637. He came to Maryland with his father and mother, and married Dorothy Neale, daughter of Captain James Neale and his wife, Anna Gill, a maid of honor of Queen Henrietta Maria; he died April 8th, 1700. Captain James Neale[69] arrived in Maryland about 1642. In 1643 he was appointed a member of the Provincial Council and a Commissioner of Lord Baltimore's Treasury. In 1660 he went to Amsterdam in Holland, deputed by Lord Baltimore to act as his attorney in regard to the trespasses of the Dutch upon that portion of Maryland bordering on Delaware Bay.[70] In 1661 he was commissioned a Captain. In the

---

[69] He belonged, apparently, to the Neales of Warnford in Hampshire. Their arms were : Argent, a fess gules in chief two crescents, in base a bugle-horn of the last straight vert: crest ; a chaplet of laurel, vert. William Berry's *County Genealogies. Hants*, page 149.

[70] Againe in the year 1660 did appeare att Amsterdam in Holland Capt James Neale being a person deputed from the Lord Baltimore protesting in the name of Caecilius Baron of Baltemore in a manner and forme

Calendar of Maryland State Papers 1660–61, appears the petition of James Neale to Charles the Second for the office of Treasurer: "He and his father lost Blood and Estate in his Majestys service and now joyfully expect his speedy return and restitution." He was a member of the Provincial Council of Maryland from 1661 to 1662;[71] he represented Charles County in 1666 in the House of Burgesses; and he died in 1684.

Roger Brooke and Dorothy Neale, his wife, had, with others, Roger Brooke who was born April 12th, 1673. He married on Feb. 23rd, 1702, Elizabeth, daughter of Francis Hutchins, member of the House of Burgesses, 1682–83, for Calvert County, and signer

as afore the deputyes had done att delaware   The Company was sitting then in the New West India House in Amsterdam where the said Iames Neale did appeare and protest by Notoriall Act of the wrong done to his Lordship by their Ministers of State in America by usurping and unlawfully possessing a Considerable part of his province of Maryland, Especially that part which was called by the Name of Delaware Bay demanding not onely the Restauration of the said Territoryes soe uniustly detained with satisfaction also for the injury his Lops hath sustained thereby." *Archives of Maryland: Proceedings of the Council of Maryland, 1667-1687-8.* Baltimore, 1887, pages 414, 415.

[71] "At a Councell held at St Marys the 12th octobr 1661

" Present The Gouernor Secretary Mr Robert Clarke Mr Baker Brooke Mr Edward LLoyd and Mr John Bateman

" Was Sworne of the Councell Captaine James Neale And after satt as a Counceller."

Archives of Maryland: Proceedings of the Council of Maryland, 1636-1667. Baltimore 1885, page 434.

of the address of the Protestant subjects of King William in August, 1689.[72]

Roger Brooke and Elizabeth Hutchins, his wife, had Roger Brooke born June 10th, 1714, who married Sarah Bowyer, a Friend, of Philadelphia.[73]

Their son, Bowyer Brooke, who was born at Philadelphia, January 25th, 1737, married August 21st, 1767, Hannah Reese, and died March 17th, 1815.

They had Bowyer Brooke, who was born at Philadelphia, December 13th, 1769, married Lydia Shinn of Burlington County, New Jersey, and died April 20th, 1838.

Their son John Bowyer Brooke of Cincinnati, Ohio, was born August 15th, 1797, and died January 21st, 1834; he married August 25th, 1831, Catherine Spayd, grand-daughter of Joseph Hiester, fifth Governor of Pennsylvania.

They had John Bowyer Brooke, of Reading, Pennsylvania, who was born April 20th, 1834, and died March 19th, 1898; he graduated at the Jefferson Medical College at Philadelphia in 1856, and married October 25th, 1860, Maria Wharton Morris of Philadel-

[72] *Archives of Maryland: Proceedings and Acts of the General Assembly of Maryland, April, 1684—June, 1692.* Baltimore 1894, pages 29, 41, 54, 96, 242.

[73] Bible and other family papers belonging to Arthur Spayd Brooke, Esq. of Reading, Pennsylvania.

phia, great-grandchild of Thomas Wharton, Governor of Pennsylvania in the time of the Revolutionary War.

Issue :

> Helen Brooke, m. Noel Wittman.
>
> Arthur Spayd Brooke, graduated at the University of Pennsylvania, 1897.

A PARTIAL INDEX.

Adison, Colonel John   . . .   . . Note 36
Alabama arbitration . . . . .   Pages 52, 53
Balch, Rev. Stephen Bloomer .   . Page 43
Baker arms . . . . Note 14
    family . . . .   Note 14
    Mary, ... Page 9
Baltimore, Lord . . . . .   Pages 14, 15, 19, 61
Beall, Anna, ... Page 43
    Eliza Ridgely, ... Page 57
    Elizabeth, ... Page 43
    First Colonel George, ... Pages 22, 33
    Second Colonel George, ... Page 37
    Colonel Ninian, ... Page 22
    Thomas Brooke,   . . . Pages 40, 42, 43 ; notes 54, 57
    Thomas, " of George "   . . . . . Pages 35, 36, 41, 57
Berkeley, Sir William, Governor of Virginia . . . . Page 17
Brooke arms . . . . Note 2 ; page 6
    Richard, ... Pages 1–4
    Robert, of London . . . . Pages 3, 4
    Robert, the emigrant . . . . . . Pages 9–16, 59, 61
    Roger, (1637–1700) . . . . Pages 12, 61
    Thomas, the first of Whitchurch . . . . Pages 3–8
    Major Thomas, ... Pages 16–18
    Colonel Thomas, ...   Pages 18–22
Calvert, Philip, ... Page 16
Charles the First . . . . Pages 2, 8, 30
    the Second . . . . Pages 30, 62
Cheshire . . . . Note 67
Columbia College . . . . Page 52
Corcoran, William W. . . . . Pages 48, 49
Dent, Barbara, ... Pages 20, 21, 22
Devonshire . . . . Page 43

A PARTIAL INDEX.

Drummond, William, Governor of the Southward Plantations . . . . Page 17
Dumbartonshire . . . . Page 22
Dumbarton, Rock of . . . . . Pages 24, 25, 28, 35 ; note 54
Dunbar, battle of . . . . Page 23
Forster of Hunsdon . . . . Page 6 ; note 6
    of Iden . . . . Note 6
    Sir Thomas, ... Pages 6, 7
Geneva Tribunal . . . . Page 53
Georgetown, D. C., Pages 33–51 *passim*, 58 ; notes 50, 54, 55, ... 57, 58, 60
Hampshire (Hants, Southampton) Pages 1, 3, 9 ; notes 1, 2, 69
Harvard . . . . Page 53
Hatton, Eleanor, ... Page 18
Inner Temple . . . . Page 7
Jackson, Andrew, ... Page 51
Liberia . . . . Pages 45, 51, 56
Magruders (McGregors) . . . . Note 54
Mainwaring arms . . . . Note 67
        Mary, ... Pages 10, 59, 61
        Roger, Bishop of St. David . . . . Page 59
Mecklenburg Declaration of Independence . . . . . Note 64
Naval Academy . . . . Page 54
Neale arms . . . . Note 69
        Captain James, ... Pages 61, 62
Oxford University . . . . Pages 5, 9
Pennsylvania, University of . . . . Page 64
Presbyterian Church, etc. . . . Pages 43, 44, 49, 55 ; note 64
Princeton College . . . . Pages 43, 50, 51, 52, 55 ; note 64
Rock of Dumbarton . . . . Pages 24, 25, 28, 35 ; note 54
Slaves, freeing . . . . Pages 45, 51
Somersetshire . . . . Page 43
Stone, William, Governor of Maryland . . . . . Pages 14, 16
Sussex . . . . Notes 6, 14 ; pages 9, 10
Taney, Roger Brooke . . . . Pages 10, 51 ; note 15
Twyne arms . . . . Note 1 ; page 6
        Elizabeth, ... Pages 1–4
Washington, Lewis William, ... Pages 58, 59
        Colonel George Corbin, ... Page 57
Wharton, Thomas, Governor of Pennsylvania . . . . Page 64
Whitchurch . . . . Pages 1, 2, 3, 5, 8, 9
Wiltshire . . . . Page 57